9781424207527

Too close for comfort

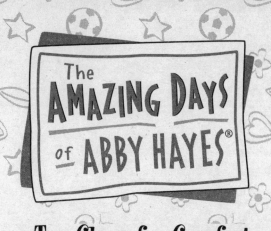

The AMAZING DAYS of ABBY HAYES®

Too Close for Comfort

ANNE MAZER

AN
APPLE
PAPERBACK

SCHOLASTIC INC.
New York Toronto London Auckland Sydney
Mexico City New Delhi Hong Kong Buenos Aires

ISBN 0-439-48273-9

Copyright © 2003 by Anne Mazer
All rights reserved. Published by Scholastic Inc.

SCHOLASTIC, APPLE PAPERBACKS, THE AMAZING DAYS OF ABBY HAYES, and associated logos are trademarks and/or registered trademarks of Scholastic Inc.

Illustrations by Monica Gesue

12 11 10 9 8 7 6 5   4 5 6 7 8/0

Printed in the U.S.A.   40

First printing, July 2003

For Joe and for Gina:
Remember the camping trips?

Chapter 1

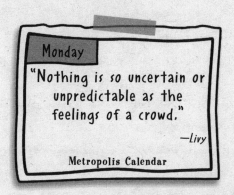

<u>Wrong!</u>

I am certain of the feelings of the crowd tonight and can predict them perfectly.

Abby's Perfect Predictions

The crowd will be celebrating. Little kids will run around, playing games. Adults will relax and laugh. A band will play. Families will grill hot dogs, hamburgers, and veggie kabobs. Everyone will watch the fireworks together and cheer.

Yes, it's the Fourth of July!!!!

Hooray for the Fourth! Hooray! <u>Hooray!</u>

Our entire family will picnic in the state park. We'll swim, play games, and go on a short hike. Before it gets dark, we'll find a good spot on the hill and wait for the fireworks to begin.

We will all be there: my mother, my father, Eva and Isabel, and Alex. And me!

Only my cat, T-Jeff, gets left behind.

It doesn't seem fair! Especially since he's named after a famous president, Thomas Jefferson.

Naming him Thomas Jefferson was Isabel's idea, not mine. She is a history buff.

A buff reminds me of something that polishes furniture or cars. Isabel never polishes anything but her fingernails. She has painted them red, white, and blue in honor of the holiday.

Sorry, T-Jeff! Even with your patriotic name, you have to stay home today.

* * *

I can't wait until we leave!! Only one
hour twenty-three minutes and fifteen seconds to go.
Fourteen seconds . . .
Thirteen . . .
Twelve . . .
Aaaaaaah! Never mind. I am going to
pack my backpack with my swimsuit, a
towel, my journal, and a book.

"You're squashing me," Alex complained to Abby.
Her seven-year-old brother wiggled an inch closer to
the car door.

"Sorry!" Abby said. "It's the picnic basket." She
tried to push it away to make room, but it was
wedged tightly and wouldn't budge.

Every free space inside the van was filled with
hampers of food, blankets and towels, tennis rackets,
Frisbees, Rollerblades and swimsuits, folding chairs
and bags of books, coolers filled with ice and soda,
and, of course, the Hayes family.

Outside, on the roof of the van, three bikes were
locked into a bike carrier.

"We have enough equipment for an army," Abby's

father, Paul Hayes, grumbled. "Or at least for several weeks in the wilderness."

"Look on the bright side," his wife, Olivia Hayes, said. "We can't possibly have forgotten *anything*. Right?"

Eva Hayes, fourteen years old, suddenly smacked her forehead and cried out. "I forgot my bathing suit!"

Her twin, Isabel, pursed her lips in a superior way. "You can wear one of mine. I brought an extra."

"A racing suit?" Eva asked.

Eva was the athletic twin. She was on the swim team, the basketball team, the softball team, and the lacrosse team.

There ought to be an Eva team, Abby thought.

"It's a bikini," Isabel announced. She waved her hand dramatically in the air. Her fingernails gleamed.

Isabel loved drama and dressing up, history and debates. She was also the president of her class.

One day she would be president of the universe, if Eva didn't beat her to it.

"You *know* I don't wear bikinis!!" Eva cried. "They're not made for serious swimming! Dad, turn around!"

Paul Hayes's sigh traveled all around the van.

"Eva, I'm not driving back for a bathing suit. Especially when your sister has an extra."

"*Mom!*" Eva wailed.

Olivia Hayes turned around. "Eva, settle down," she said. "If you don't want to wear a bikini, then don't swim. Simple."

"What color is it?" Eva asked.

"Purple," said Isabel.

Eva frowned.

"Hooray for purple!" Abby said. It was her favorite color. She had painted her room entirely in purple. And her furniture. She had even hung purple curtains to match her purple bedspread. Some members of the Hayes family said that being in Abby's room was like being inside a giant grape.

"I'm sure the suit will fit you, Eva," Isabel continued.

"Oh, shut up!" Eva said.

"No fights while I'm driving," Paul Hayes said. "Let's change the subject."

"Yes, let's," his wife agreed. "I heard — and did — enough arguing this week at work." Olivia Hayes was a lawyer.

"You get paid to argue," Isabel pointed out.

"If Eva and Isabel got paid, they'd earn a fortune," Abby said under her breath.

Isabel turned around in her seat. "Say that again?"

"You'd make a great lawyer," Abby said sincerely.

"Thanks!" Isabel flashed the smile that had gotten her elected to Student Council every year since second grade.

"*I* wouldn't hire you!" Eva slumped in her seat, sulking.

"What about our camping trip?" Paul Hayes said in a hearty voice. "Let's talk about our trip to the mountains."

"We're leaving in less than a week," Olivia Hayes reminded everyone.

"Eva and I are setting up our own tent this year!" Isabel announced.

Her twin smiled at her, for once.

"We're bringing only one tent," Paul Hayes warned her, "good old Château Hayes."

"Oh, no!" Alex groaned. "Last year I woke up every morning with Isabel's feet in my face!"

"That's why Eva and I decided to stay in our own tent," Isabel said. "I'm picking it up tomorrow."

"No, *I* am," Eva said.

"*I* arranged it," Isabel said.

"It looks like there'll be lots of room in Château

Hayes this year," their father interrupted. "Alex and Abby, do either of you want to invite a friend?"

Alex shook his head.

"I do!" Abby cried. "Can we have our own tent, too?"

Abby's father was quiet for a moment.

"You're old enough," he said finally. "Ask the neighbors if you can borrow their two-person tent."

"Why don't you invite Jessica?" her mother suggested. "She's returning this week."

Abby's best friend had spent the past few months living with her father and his family in Oregon.

"Uh, no," Abby said. "Probably not."

"How come you don't want to invite your best friend?" Eva asked.

Abby shrugged. She didn't want to explain.

While she was in Oregon, Jessica had turned into Jessy.

Once, Jessica had loved science, drawing, and hanging out with Abby and Natalie. Now Jessy only wanted to go to parties, wear trendy clothes, and talk about boys. She didn't answer Abby's e-mails very often.

"Jessica will want to spend time with her mother,"

Paul Hayes said. "They haven't seen each other in months."

"Yes," Abby agreed.

"Invite her anyway," Eva suggested. "You never know."

Paul Hayes slowed the van and pulled into the turn lane. "Abby can invite anyone she wants."

"Okay," Abby said. She smiled at her father. He always seemed to understand.

"I have lots of friends," she added. Her mind quickly scrolled through the possibilities. Her cousin Cleo lived hundreds of miles away. So did her new friend, Mira. Bethany was at farm camp. Natalie was taking a drama course. Casey was a boy. Brianna was impossible.

Well, she would find someone to invite. Somewhere.

"Here we are," Olivia Hayes said. The van pulled into a long line of cars waiting to enter the parking lot.

"There's Aaron!" Eva cried, pointing to a tall boy wearing orange swim trunks and carrying a large cooler. She rolled down the window and called out his name.

He turned to wave.

"I'm getting out," Eva announced. She slid open the van door and hopped down. Aaron smiled as he saw her head toward him.

"She doesn't help us unload the van," Isabel grumbled. "As usual!"

"No fair!" Alex complained, picking up his cue from Isabel.

"Let Eva be," their father said. "She'll help out later."

Abby scanned the parking lot. She saw hundreds of cars as well as people carrying coolers, chairs, and blankets. Not a familiar face in sight. Abby hoped that she, too, like Eva, would find a friend soon.

Chapter 2

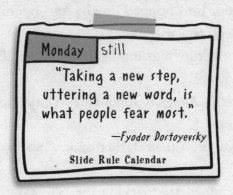

Monday | still

"Taking a new step,
uttering a new word, is
what people fear most."

—Fyodor Dostoyevsky

Slide Rule Calendar

I have to take a new step. The step is made of concrete. My feet will be bare. I will be wearing a new lavender bathing suit. Even though it's just a step into the swimming pool, I fear it a lot.

I have to utter a new word, too. Even though I've said it millions of times in my life, I'm afraid to say "hello."

<u>Nine Reasons for Being Terrified of a Concrete Step and the Word "Hello"</u>

1. The step leads into the water.
2. In the water is a group of girls.

3. The girls look like they're my age.
4. They're playing Marco Polo.
5. They're splashing and yelling and laughing.
6. They look like they're having a lot of fun.
7. I want to play Marco Polo with them.
8. I have to say hello first.
9. I'm afraid to introduce myself to a group of girls I don't know.

What will they do? Will they act like they don't see me? Will they say no? Will they laugh at me? Will they stop playing and leave? Or will they invite me to join them?

Help!

Three Wishes

1. I wish my journal would hold my hand.
2. I wish my journal would reassure me the way Jessica used to do.
3. I wish my journal would give me advice and write me back once in a while.

One More Wish

I wish my journal was my friend. Then I wouldn't need to make new friends.

I'm the only one in the Hayes family with no one to talk to or play with at the Fourth of July picnic. Alex found one of his friends. Isabel joined Eva and Aaron. I'm all alone!!

Two Choices

1. Take new step and say new word. (Will put self in the <u>Hayes Book of World Records</u> for surviving the Ordeal of Ordinary Objects.)
2. Or wait to see if friend or schoolmate shows up. Otherwise swim alone, swing on bars alone, and bike on paths alone. Pretend I like it.

A Decision

I will do what I fear most. Okay, here goes. Really. I mean it. I will step into the icy pool and approach the girls. I will close *my journal, put away my purple pen, and stop writing nowwwwwwww. . . .*

Abby carefully put her journal into her backpack. She picked up her towel and swim goggles. "I'm going swimming, Mom!"

Her mother was unpacking bags of chips and cans of soda and piling them onto the picnic table. "Have a good time, honey!" she said, glancing up and smiling.

Abby walked slowly toward the water.

At the edge of the grass, she spread out her towel and slipped off her sandals. Then she picked her way across the ground to the concrete steps. She dangled one foot in the water, then stepped lower.

The water was cool but not icy. Her heart was pounding. To calm herself, she took a deep breath.

"Marco! Polo! Marco! Polo!" The girls' shouts echoed against the rock walls that surrounded the pool.

"You cheated!" someone yelled.

"Did not!"

Everyone laughed.

Abby ducked under the water and gasped from the

cold. She swam out and emerged near the girls playing Marco Polo.

She didn't *have* to talk to them. She could simply stand here and watch.

"Look out, Hannah!" someone yelled.

A tall, thin girl was swimming rapidly toward Abby. Before Abby could get out of the way, the girl surfaced right next to her.

"That was close," the girl said. "I almost crashed into you." She gestured toward her friends. "We're playing Marco Polo."

"Yes," Abby said, staring at the girl.

Her hair was in a braid down her back. Her teeth were a little crooked. Her arms and legs looked like they were too long for her body. She was wearing a faded halter-top bathing suit. Her smile was friendly and her eyes sparkled. "Hannah!" someone called.

Hannah smiled again at Abby and disappeared under the water.

"Marco! Polo! Polo!"

Suddenly, Hannah reemerged. "Hey!" she said.

Abby took a breath.

"Want to join us?" Hannah asked. "I'm Hannah."

She didn't wait for a reply. "Come on!" she urged, jumping back underwater.

Abby dove after her.

<u>News Flash!!!! An Up-to-the-Minute Bulletin and July Fourth News Report</u>

Abby Hayes, age ten, took a bold step today. She joined a group of girls she didn't know and played Marco Polo with them.

It was a lot of fun.

The girls were friendly, and later they invited her to play with them on the jungle gym. Then Abby, Hannah, and a girl named Sophie hiked to a waterfall together.

Abby thought Sophie was really nice, but Hannah was <u>great</u>!!!

Hannah never stops talking. She has millions of ideas. She is excited about everything. She loves to read and write (hooray!), she loves bugs, and frogs, and birds, and waterfalls, and plants, and chocolate mint ice cream, and all the colors of the rainbow, and Rollerblading (double hooray!),

and sleepovers with friends
(triple hooray!), and singing,
and playing cards, and —

This list is interrupted because there is
not enough time or space or energy to write
<u>everything</u> that Hannah loves.

After the hike, Hannah invited Abby to
meet her family.

Hannah has a little sister, Elena. Elena is
a year and a half old. She has short
chubby legs and fat cheeks. She walks like
a little windup toy. She is so <u>cute</u>!!!

(Your roving reporter, Abby Hayes, wants
a little sister, too!!!)

Hannah's father is from England. It's
hard to understand his accent sometimes. He
is a high school biology teacher. Hannah's
mother was born in Ohio. She is a grade
school teacher.

Abby Hayes asked Hannah's family to
meet her family. Everyone liked one another.
They decided to picnic and watch the fireworks together.

● ● ●

Extra!!! The Best, Most Exciting News on the Planet, IN THE SOLAR SYSTEM, AND POSSIBLY THE ENTIRE UNIVERSE

An extraordinary discovery was made right before the fireworks display.

It started off with a boring conversation between adults. Abby's father asked Hannah's mother where she taught. Hannah's mother, Susan, said that last year she taught in a rural district but now had transferred to a city school. Next year she will teach kindergarten at Lancaster Elementary — my school!!!!!

Our roving reporter was breathless from the wonderful news. She couldn't say a word.

"And what about Hannah?" Olivia Hayes asked. "Will she be at Lancaster Elementary, too?"

Hannah's father, Michael, said that Hannah was enrolled in Ms. Kantor's class. That's my class!!!!!

The family plans to move at the end of the summer. They will either rent or buy a house. Paul and Olivia Hayes offered to

help them find something in our neighborhood.

We interrupt this news bulletin to jump for joy, turn a cart-wheel in the grass (no room, too many picnickers), and shout with happiness.

The fireworks were bigger and better than ever.

But the news about Hannah and her family was more a) dramatic; b) exciting; c) thrilling; and d) spectacular than any fireworks.

The news made everyone happy. Especially Abby and Hannah.

Chapter 3

Really???

<u>Abby's Thoughts (in numerical order)</u>
1st thought. To invite Hannah
to go camping with us!

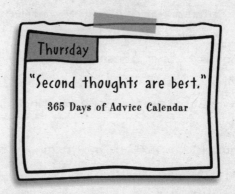

I whispered this thought to
my parents after the fireworks display.
They thought that my thought was a
great thought.
<u>I invited Hannah, and she is coming!</u>

The next morning I had a second

thought: It's one thing to spend the Fourth of July with a wonderful new friend and another to spend a whole week with her.

3rd thought. She doesn't know my family very well.

4th thought. What if she doesn't like my family?

5th thought. What if my family does something embarrassing?

6th thought. What if Hannah decides she doesn't like me?

7th thought. What if Hannah really can't stand me or my family?

8th thought. If Hannah and I don't get along, we'll still have to spend the entire week together.

9th thought. Wouldn't it have been safer to get to know each other slowly?

10th thought. The second thought was not the best! It was the worst, because it led to a lot of worries.

11th thought. I don't like my thoughts.

12th thought. Can I have second thoughts about my twelve thoughts?

13th thought. QUIT WHILE YOU'RE AHEAD!!

Decided to stop thinking.

Went into Isabel's room. She was writing a story. This summer she is taking a creative writing course called Finding Your Voice: A Workshop for Today's Teens.

(Why does she need help finding it? Isabel's voice is very loud!)

I asked her for help.

Isabel: Don't worry so much!

Me: What will Hannah think when you and Eva start fighting???

Isabel: She's seen fights before.

Me: Oh, yeah? Her sister is one and a half. Her parents are really nice. She's not used to all-out war.

Isabel: She'll roll with it.

Me: How do you know?

Isabel: Abby, lighten up.

Me: Will you and Eva try not to fight? Please? Please?

Isabel (sighs): We don't _plan_ to fight, you know.

Me: Plan to get along, then!

I went to see Eva. She wasn't finding her voice, she was losing her stomach.

(_What_ stomach? Eva is trim and fit because she exercises all the time!)

Eva (panting from exertion): I have to stay in shape. Or else!

Me: Will you do weird exercises while we're on vacation?

Eva: Calisthenics, yoga, and tai chi aren't weird, Abby.

Me: Whatever. Just don't embarrass me in front of Hannah, okay?

Eva: Maybe Hannah will join me. I'll ask her.

Me: _NO!!!_

I ran out of the room and went to find Alex. He was playing in the living room. He was in his pajamas. It was three o'clock in the afternoon.

* * *

Alex: My space monsters are invincible!

Me: Alex, please don't wear pajamas all day long when we're camping.

Alex: Why not?

Me: Because Hannah will be there.

Alex: So?

Me: It's embarrassing!

Alex: When I go camping, I don't <u>ever</u> change my clothes. Or brush my teeth.

Me: AAAAAAAAARRRRRRGGGGHH!

HOW MUCH CAN MY FAMILY EMBARRASS ME? LET ME COUNT THE WAYS.

There are <u>too many</u> ways that my family can embarrass me!

Decided to present a petition at dinner to my entire family.

<u>Abby's Dinnertime Proclamation</u>

Me: Hear ye! Hear ye!

Paul Hayes: We're all ears.

Alex: What about eyes and nose and mouth?

Eva: Very funny, Alex.

Isabel: Don't make fun of him.

Eva: I <u>wasn't</u> making fun of him, Ms. Know-It-All!

Isabel: Listen, Muscle Girl —

Me (louder): Hear ye! Hear ye! I mean, hear me! Hear <u>ME</u>!

Olivia Hayes: We're listening, honey.

Me: I hereby present to you the Hayes Peace Proclamation.

I unrolled a piece of purple parchment tied with a bit of leftover string and held it up in front of my entire family.

Paul Hayes: The Hayes Peace Proclamation? What's this?

Eva: I'm not signing anything without a lawyer present.

Isabel (sarcastic): <u>Cute</u>, Eva.

Alex: We always have a lawyer around the house! Mom!

Olivia Hayes: That's right, honey.

Me: Will you please <u>listen</u>??

Paul Hayes takes the purple parchment

from me, shushes everyone, and reads aloud.

"We, the undersigned members of the Hayes family, do solemnly declare that we will not fight, shout, make bad jokes, wear pajamas all day long, forget to change clothing, burp loudly and then laugh, fight, sing silly songs, tell embarrassing stories about Abby when she was younger, argue about stupid things, fight, sulk, yell, or pout, chew with mouth open, forget to brush teeth, cut toenails in public, fight, gulp food, drink directly from milk or juice carton, or eat with fingers. Or fight.

"This declaration will be valid from the time that Hannah arrives to the time that she leaves the Hayes family camping trip.

"Witnessed this day of July . . ."

Paul Hayes: This is quite a document. You wrote it yourself?

Me: Yes.

Eva: You're crazy if you think _this_ family will sign _that_ document.

Isabel: You've taken all the fun out of camping! I mean, the whole point is to leave civilization behind and act natural.

Olivia Hayes: Don't you think you've gone a bit overboard, Abby? Hannah is used to her own family. I'm sure they burp and argue once in a while.

Me: Will you sign it or not?

Everyone: <u>NO!</u>

Me (in tiny voice): At least you all agree.

Paul Hayes: Sorry, Abby. We'll try not to embarrass you. I'm sure Hannah will tolerate us. We're a likable bunch, aren't we?

Suddenly, I surprised and embarrassed <u>myself</u> by bursting into tears.

Me (in a very tiny voice): Jessica doesn't like me anymore; Natalie and Bethany like each other better than me; Cleo lives far away. I have no close friends anymore!!! <u>NO ONE!</u>

The entire Hayes family sat in shocked silence. Then Paul Hayes took out a pen and signed the Peace Proclamation. He handed it to his wife, who was next to sign. One by one, Eva, Isabel, and Alex signed it, too. Silently, they handed it back to me.

Chapter 4

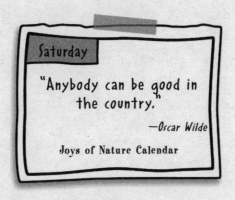

Saturday

"Anybody can be good in the country."

—Oscar Wilde

Joys of Nature Calendar

I hope this is 100 percent true!
It <u>better</u> be!!

Hannah <u>must</u> get a positive impression of the Hayes family!

If my family keeps their promise, I will reward them with eternal gratitude. I will let my siblings watch their favorite television programs, without complaining or saying how stupid they are, for a year. My parents will not have to nag me to do chores <u>ever</u> <u>again</u>.

The van sped toward the mountains. Traffic was heavy. It looked as if the entire world was going on vacation.

"We're making a rest stop," Olivia Hayes announced. She was at the wheel. In the seat next to her, her husband had fallen asleep with a baseball cap over his face.

No one answered.

Eva and Isabel were connected to individual CD players. They each swayed in time to their music. To everyone else, it sounded like a loud metallic buzz.

Behind the twins sat Abby, Hannah, and Alex. Alex was reading a comic book. Abby and Hannah were talking quietly together.

"My sisters look like identical aliens," Abby said to Hannah. "Hooked up to space-age music machines."

Hannah grinned. She was wearing yellow Capri pants and a polka-dotted T-shirt. "Maybe the music controls them," she replied. "Maybe it programs their thoughts."

"Beep, beep, bleep!" Abby said. "Bip, bip, blip!"

"Do I hear intelligent conversation in the universe?" Paul Hayes said, sitting up and taking the baseball cap off his face.

"You're awake," his wife said. "Just in time." She pulled off the highway and parked the car.

Abby pulled out her journal. Her sisters unplugged themselves. Her brother dropped his comic book on the floor.

Hannah picked up her backpack.

The entire family piled out of the van.

So far, so good. Hayes family on best behavior.

The family has refrained from singing silly songs badly together, as they usually do on car trips.

They have refrained from complaining and arguing.

No one has burped, flossed their teeth in the van, or made bathroom jokes.

A few close calls at the rest stop.

1. Getting out of van, Alex cried that he "had to go"!
"Alex!" I hissed.

"I mean, I have to go <u>run</u>." He sprinted toward the rest station.

"It's good to run after you've been cooped up in a car," I said to Hannah.

2. Isabel bought a chocolate bar from one of the vending machines.

"Aren't you going to give me a piece?" Eva asked.

"No way!" Isabel cried, then caught my eye. "I mean, that's no way to keep in shape, Eva. You have to remember your team."

Eva was about to retort angrily, but I nudged her.

"You're so kind, Isabel, dear," Eva said instead, "putting my interests above your own."

"No problem, Eva, darling," Isabel replied. "You come first."

Hannah stared at them.

"My sisters are always thinking of each other," I said.

3. Hannah went into the rest room.

A few minutes later, my mother and Eva began yoga stretches on the grass.

People stared curiously at my mother and sister. My sister was upside down. My mother was twisted like a pretzel.

"Dad! Make them stop!" I cried. "Quick! Before Hannah shows up!"

My father shook his head. "Sorry, Abby," he said. "Driving a long distance takes its toll. I'm going to join them."

Before I could even argue, my dad was stretched out on the grass with his legs backward over his head.

I rushed into the rest room. Hannah was washing her hands.

"Don't leave without me!" I begged.

"Sure, I'll wait." Hannah took a stick of gum from her backpack and popped it into her mouth.

I pulled out my purple hairbrush and brushed – and brushed – and brushed – and brushed – and brushed – and brushed – and brushed – and bru –

"Do you always brush your hair this much, Abby?"

"Just on trips."

"It's perfect already."

"Once more —"

When we got out, I was relieved to see my entire family with feet firmly on ground and heads in normal place.

"I had to brush my hair," I explained. "See?" I patted my usually wild, messy red curls. Now they were <u>un</u>usually neat and smooth.

"Very nice," my father said with a smile. "Now get in the van."

<u>SAVED!!!!</u> By the brush!!!

"There are state parks," Paul Hayes said, "and then there are *state parks*. *This* is one of the best in the Northeast," he announced as he drove into the park entrance.

"We're finally here!" his wife exclaimed.

The long, winding drive was bordered with tall pine trees. "Everything smells wonderful, doesn't it?"

Abby's father raved. "The lake, the pine trees, the fresh air. And our favorite campsite is waiting for us."

"Wait until you see it, Hannah," Olivia Hayes said, turning around to face the girls. "It overlooks the water, it's very private and sheltered, *and* it's near the bathrooms and shower."

"You mean the comfort station," Abby corrected.

Olivia Hayes sighed. "Yes, near the *comfort station*."

"You don't want to walk half a mile in the middle of the night," Isabel pointed out.

"No!" Hannah agreed.

"Especially not when your flashlight dies or when you hear weird growling noises in the woods," Eva began.

"Oh, come on, Eva," Isabel interrupted. "Don't scare Hannah!"

"I'm not scared," Hannah said.

"You've had a lot of camping experiences, then?" Paul Hayes asked.

"No," Hannah said cheerfully. "This is my first one."

There was a moment of silence. Then Isabel and Eva cried out in unison.

"Your first time camping??? With *us*?!"

"Uh-oh," Alex said.

"It'll be *great*!" Abby cried.

Paul Hayes pulled up to the park office. "Yes, it will. Hannah, we're very happy to have you with us."

"Thank you," Hannah said with a big smile. "I know I'll love it."

At the park office, a park ranger behind the desk greeted them. "You have reservations?" he asked. "We're booked."

"We made a reservation in advance," Paul Hayes replied. "Under the name of Hayes. Site 127. Our favorite," he added.

"That's a nice one," the ranger agreed, typing on the computer. "Which credit card did you use?"

"Visa," Paul said. "Or maybe it was my Master-Card?"

"That's H-a-y-s?" the ranger said. "Or do you spell it with a 'z'?"

"H-a-y-e-s," Olivia said.

"I'm not showing anything," the ranger said with a frown, scanning the computer screen. He typed rapidly on the keyboard. "In fact, we have a Levitt family in 127. When did you make the reservation?"

"Six months ago," Paul Hayes said. Then he stopped. "I'm *sure* I did. At least I think I did. I know I did! I *had* to. Or did I? Could I have —"

"Did you receive an e-mail confirmation?" the ranger asked.

Paul Hayes shook his head.

"Then you probably didn't make a reservation," the ranger concluded.

"Strange." Paul frowned. "I could have sworn —"

He pulled out some papers, scanned them quickly, then stuffed them back in his pocket. "I do it every single year," he said.

"Paul," Olivia Hayes interrupted. "Don't tell me —"

Abby's father sighed. "I'm afraid it's true."

"We don't have a reservation?!" she cried out. "You *forgot*?"

"I'm sorry," he replied miserably.

"We've been driving seven hours with five kids, haven't eaten dinner yet, and have nowhere to spend the night?"

"No problem, no problem," Paul said with a soothing gesture of his hands. "We'll work it out."

"*Work it out?*" Olivia snapped. "It's almost dark! Where and what are we going to eat? Where will we set up the tents? What about our *carefully* planned vacation?"

Eva and Isabel exchanged glances with Abby and Alex.

"She's in her courtroom mode," Eva muttered. "Watch out."

"Are there any camping grounds nearby?" Paul asked the ranger. "Or is there another state park within driving distance?"

"They're booked up, too," the ranger said. "I don't know what to tell you, folks. It's our busy season. The hotels and lodges are full, too."

Olivia Hayes stepped forward. "Do you ever get cancellations? We'll take anything."

The ranger scratched his head. "Let me see." He typed a few more words, sighed, and clicked the mouse.

"Thank you very much," Olivia said.

She turned again to her husband. Her voice was far less friendly. "I don't plan to spend the night in the van."

Abby held her breath. Next to her, Alex was rubbing his face — his way of showing that he was upset.

What if they all had to sleep in the van? What if her parents had a nasty fight in public? Would Hannah still be her friend?

Abby looked to her twin sisters for help. They were staring at the floor.

Suddenly, Isabel straightened up. "Don't worry, Mom," she said, putting her arm around her mother's shoulders. "Whatever happens, we can handle it. Right, Eva?"

"*Right!*" Eva said, giving her twin a thumbs-up. "What do you think, team?" she said to Abby, Alex, and Hannah.

Abby shot a grateful look at both of her sisters. "We can handle it," she said more bravely than she felt. "Can't we, Alex?"

Alex blinked at his sisters. "Sure," he said. "I guess."

"Hannah?" Isabel asked.

"Wow. Sleeping in a van," Hannah said. Her eyes were wide. "That'd be an adventure!"

Abby gazed at her new friend in admiration. Hannah really did have a good attitude. No matter what, she *always* had a smile on her face.

The ranger looked up from his computer. "You

folks are in luck," he said. "Let me double-check. Yes, it looks like we just had a cancellation. Do you want it?"

"Yes!" Paul Hayes said hastily. "Wherever and whatever it is. Can we have it for a week?"

"Let me see," the ranger replied. He clicked the mouse a few more times. "Yes, there's a week available."

The entire family sighed with relief.

Paul Hayes handed his credit card to the ranger and began to write the family's name and address on a registration form.

"All's well that ends well," Olivia said, letting out a long breath and managing a smile.

Abby crossed her fingers. She hoped that what her mother said was true.

Chapter 5

Small is squashed.
Small is inconvenient.
Small is tight.
Small is crowded.
Small is noisy.
Small is . . .

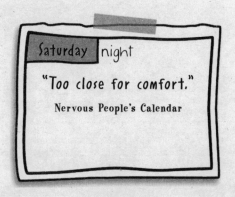

It's a two-in-one quote day!

Small is too close for comfort. That's for sure!

Ha!

The Hayes campsite is so small that all of our tents are bumping against one another.

We can hear one another breathe. We can hear one another whisper. We can hear Dad snore!

Our campsite is also surrounded by other campsites. They are next to us, behind us, across from us, and around us.

We can hear other people talking, sneezing, laughing, cooking, washing pots, playing music, and starting their cars.

It's noisier than a city!!!!!!

This isn't the great wilderness, it's a tent and camper convention! (With a few pine trees added for scenery.)

Site 127 isn't like this at all!! It is pri-

vate, quiet, spacious, and peaceful. How
did Dad forget to make the reservation??

On Sunday morning, Hannah rolled out of her sleeping bag, already smiling.

"Do you smile in your sleep?" Abby asked.

"That's what my mother says." Hannah folded her pajamas and put them under her pillow. "I never stop talking, and I never stop smiling."

"Uhhhnnn," Abby mumbled, pulling the sleeping bag over her face. "It was so noisy last night."

The campsite next to theirs had had a party. It had gone on until late into the night.

"It was great!" Hannah said enthusiastically. "I loved the singing. And the smell and sound of the crackling fire. Do you think they were roasting marshmallows?"

She didn't wait for an answer.

"Abby, this is *soooooo* cool," Hannah said. "I never knew so many people camped out like this."

"Yeah," Abby said in reply. "And they're all *right here*."

"We'll get to know them!" Hannah said excitedly. "Maybe there'll be kids our age."

"Maybe."

"And we can have our own marshmallow roast and songfest."

"Uhhhnnnn," Abby groaned again. She didn't want to think about a songfest with her family. She didn't want to think about her family at all. There was no telling what might happen with six Hayeses living in close quarters for seven days.

"I really like your family," Hannah said.

"You *do*?" Abby's eyes opened wide.

"They're great," Hannah said.

Abby sighed deeply. "Good," she said. If Hannah liked her family, that meant she liked *her*. Didn't it?

"Stay together!" Olivia Hayes cautioned Abby and Hannah. "Don't split up, even to go to the bathroom."

"*Mom!*" Abby protested.

"You know what I mean," Olivia said.

"We won't lose sight of each other," Hannah promised. She reached into her bag and pulled out a yellow sun hat.

"Remember to reapply sunscreen after you swim," Olivia warned. "Listen to the lifeguard, and don't accept rides in boats or cars from *anyone*."

"Not even you or Dad?" Abby said.

Her mother didn't smile. "You're going to the lake by yourselves," she said. "I hope you're mature enough to behave responsibly. You have my cell phone number in case of an emergency?"

"*Yes*, Mom," Abby said.

"And you brought snacks?"

Hannah nodded. "Granola bars, peanut butter sandwiches, and juice boxes," she recited.

Her mother gave Abby a quick hug and then gave Hannah one, too. "We'll join you soon," she said. "Be safe and careful!"

"Phew," Abby said as they walked away from the campsite. "I thought she was going to make us sign something first!"

Hannah giggled. "My mom is the same way. But she's even more careful than yours."

"Really?" Abby said. "Even though she's a teacher and knows all about kids? Or *because* she's a teacher?"

"It's because I'm the oldest," Hannah explained. "Parents are always more nervous with the first child. The second one has it easier."

"I never thought about that," Abby said.

Did that mean that her older sisters had done all

the hard work for her? Was there actually an advantage to being a middle child?

"You're lucky to be second — or third," Hannah said, as if reading her thoughts. She opened her arms wide, gesturing to the campgrounds, the pine trees, the trailers and tents. "And I'm lucky to be *here*!"

For a while the girls walked in silence along the sandy road.

"If you wished for anything, what would it be?" Abby asked as they approached the swimming area.

Hannah thought. "Pierced ears," she finally said.

"*Me, too!*" Abby cried. "I can't believe you want them, too!"

"I've wanted them *forever*! But my mother —"

"— *won't let me*," Abby finished. "Mine, neither."

The two girls stopped in the middle of the road.

"Just look at these poor earlobes!" Hannah cried. "Don't you think they look cold and miserable without silver earrings covering them?"

"They're going to get a chill from the wind," Abby warned. "You better get a doctor's note."

"Yes!" Hannah agreed. "'Please make sure that Hannah has her ears properly covered by earrings in all weather. Otherwise I will not be responsible for the consequences.'"

"Earrings prevent earaches," Abby announced. "A medical fact brought to you by the *Journal of Earrings*."

"I want a subscription!" Hannah said.

Laughing, the two girls ran down the road to the beach.

After spreading out their things on a beach towel, they swam out to the dock. They dived off the board, swam back to shallow water, and practiced underwater handstands. When their hands began to turn blue, they got out and lay on towels in the sun.

Hannah sat up and rummaged in her bag. "I brought some candy," she said, throwing Abby a bag of chocolates. "One for you, one for me. I brought two of everything."

"You're the greatest!" Abby cried.

Hannah looked pleased. "Thanks for inviting me. It would have been awful at home."

"*Really?*" Abby found that hard to believe. "Your parents are so nice!"

"They used to be," Hannah said. "But lately all we do is pack. And look for a place to live. One day, I wrapped glasses and cups in newspapers for three hours! And when I'm not packing, my mother makes me take care of Elena so *she* can pack."

Abby sighed in sympathy. Even though she loved Alex, she wouldn't like to take care of him. She couldn't even imagine baby-sitting an eighteen-month-old!

"Do you have to change diapers?" Abby asked.

"Yes!" Hannah cried. "I'm so glad I'm here with you!"

Hannah's enthusiasm was contagious. It was like a reverse flu, Abby thought.

Hannah got out a deck of cards and began to shuffle. "Do you know how to play Crazy Eights?" she asked.

"Yes," Abby replied. "I used to play all the time with my best fr —" She was just about to tell Hannah about Jessica. She was just about to ask whether Hannah had a best friend and confide that she no longer had one.

"Abby Hayes!" It was a voice that she heard often during the school year. It was a voice that frequently bragged, boasted, and claimed to be best. "What are you doing here?"

"Brianna????" Abby said. "What are *you* doing here? Are you camping?"

It was hard — no, impossible — to imagine Brianna, the most fashionable girl in the fifth grade, sleeping in a tent, using public bathrooms, or cooking stew over an open fire.

"Of course not!" Brianna said with an airy wave of her hand. "We're on the island. My mother's aunt's cousin's stepdaughter owns a summerhouse there."

"The island?" Hannah said breathlessly. "You're living on an *island*?"

"Of course," Brianna said. "It's our own island. I'm Brianna," she said to Hannah, as if everyone ought to know who she was. "And you are — ?"

"Hannah."

Abby stood up and brushed sand from her hands. "Hannah's moving to our neighborhood. She'll be in Ms. Kantor's class with us."

"That's great," Brianna said. Then she added, "She'll be in class with *me*."

"And with Abby," Hannah said with a smile.

"What are you doing this summer?" Abby asked Brianna.

"Shopping," Brianna answered. "And speaking French, starring in plays, and auditioning for commercials."

"Cool!" Hannah said. "I love plays."

"This summer I won the Promising Young Talent award," Brianna bragged.

"Where's Victoria?" Abby tried to change the subject before Brianna started a marathon brag-a-thon.

"Victoria is Brianna's best friend," she explained to Hannah.

"At dance camp," Brianna said. "She might visit us on the island. I'll let you know."

"Thanks." Abby made a mental note to stay away if she did. Victoria was one of the meanest girls in their class.

"Would you like to join us for a ride on our boat?" Brianna offered. "It's a powerful motorboat, one of the best new models on the market."

"I don't —" Abby began.

"I'd *love* to ride in a motorboat!" Hannah cried. "I've never been —" She stopped and glanced at Abby. "Do you think your mother would let us?"

"My father is a very safe boat operator," Brianna said. "He's the best."

"I don't know where my mother is," Abby said. "We can't get on the boat without her permission." She tried to look sorry. "Another time, maybe."

"What's her cell number?" Brianna asked impatiently. She pulled a shiny blue phone from her purse and switched it on. "She *does* have a cell phone, doesn't she?"

"Yes," Abby admitted. Reluctantly, she recited the number. She hoped that her mother had turned off her phone.

"Hello?" her mother said.

With a sinking feeling, Abby listened as Brianna spoke to Mrs. Hayes.

"Call my father on his cell," Brianna said to Abby's mother. "He'll tell you all . . ." She made a thumbs-up sign. "Okay? They can go?"

"YES!" Hannah cried.

Abby groaned inwardly.

Brianna was the most popular girl in the fifth grade. She had huge closets of clothes. She had pierced ears. She had her own television. She had *been* on television.

She had a summerhouse on an island and a sleek new motorboat.

How could the Hayes family compete?

Chapter 6

Sunday

"Friendship redoubleth joys
and cutteth griefs
in halves."

—Francis Bacon

Kitchen Cutlery Calendar

Who knoweth what this meaneth? Isabel understandeth all this stuff, but she hiketh at a nature preserve with Alex today.

Did I writeth the quote wrong? Shouldn't it be, "Friendship redoubleth griefs and cutteth joys in halves?"

Or, as Victoria, Brianna's best friend, might say, "It's, like, you know, friends are, like, a pain when they won't, like, lend you the shirt they just bought at the coolest store in the mall, and when they, like, complain all the time that you copied their, like, math answers, and when they borrow your, you know, best necklace and forget to give it back."

Or when you have to watch the person you hoped might be your new best friend enjoy a boat ride with Brianna and her family.

That <u>really</u> cutteth the joys in half. And redoubleth the griefs.

Why did Hannah have to have such a good time? <u>How could she???</u>

The Brianna Family

1. Father: dressed like boat captain in white shorts, blue T-shirt, and sunglasses. Steered boat. Polite conversation.

2. Mother: dressed like fashion model in black silk pants and white halter top. Finger- and toenails painted gold. Read magazine. No conversation.

3. Brianna: dressed like teenage pop star

in red bikini, matching sandals, and wraparound sunglasses. Brianna-centered conversation.

The Boat

1. New
2. Sleek
3. Expensive
4. Fast
5. Powerful

Length of ride: 55 minutes

Number of brags per minute: 24

Seasickness suffered: none

Bragsickness suffered: extreme

Times Hannah smiled on ride: a billion or so

Times Hannah _didn't_ smile on ride: 0

Times Hannah laughed: 579

Times Hannah said, "This is great!": 181

Times Hannah said, "I never want this to end": 5

Times Hannah said, "I'm SO lucky!": 17

Times Abby smiled on ride: 0

Times Abby <u>didn't</u> smile on ride: a billion or so

Times Abby laughed: 0

Times Abby said, "This is great!": 0

Times Abby said, "I never want this to end": 0

Times Abby said, "I'm SO lucky!": 0

Joys: Cutteth into little, bitty, broken pieces.

Griefs: Redoubleth a few dozen times.

Surprising, Unfortunate End to Boat Ride

Hannah hugged Brianna.

Extremely Surprising Response

Brianna hugged her back.

Brianna said, "Great to meet you!"

Brianna said, "I'm glad you're in our class."

Brianna said, "Maybe we can get together later this week."

* * *

BRIANNA SPOKE THREE SENTENCES IN A ROW WITHOUT A SINGLE BRAG???

Possible Reasons Why Brianna Acted Like a Normal Human Being for the First Time in Recorded History

1. No explanation
2. There's a full moon tonight.
3. A mystery of the universe
4. A freak of nature
5. Once every seven years, Brianna acts normal, and we just happened to be there.
6. It wasn't Brianna on the boat but her non-evil twin.
7. Hannah brings out the best in people.

Questions

Does Hannah like Brianna better than me?

Does she like me better than Brianna?

Or does she like both of us?? (How could she?)

Or does she really like Brianna better but is too polite to tell me?

Who does Hannah like and why???

Hannah might be happy, but I'm not! I'm frustrated, confused, bewildered, and upset.

Chapter 7

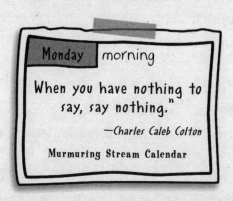

Monday morning

When you have nothing to
say, say nothing."

—Charles Caleb Colton

Murmuring Stream Calendar

"Dad, you better not burn the oatmeal this morning," Eva grumbled as she joined the Hayes family around the picnic table.

"Good news!" Paul Hayes said cheerfully. "We're not having oatmeal. It's French toast, cooked over a fire under the open sky. You'll be able to taste the fresh air, and the wood smoke, and the scent of the pines."

"Forget that; I just want plain, ordinary French toast," Isabel interrupted rudely.

"Your father got up at dawn to make the fire and start breakfast," Olivia Hayes said. "Don't you think he deserves thanks?"

"I got up at dawn and went back to bed," Isabel muttered.

"*I* jogged four miles," Eva said.

"You would," Isabel retorted.

Abby tried to kick her sisters under the table but stubbed her toe on a tree root instead. It was already that kind of day. It had been that kind of day since yesterday, when she set foot on Brianna's boat.

"Isn't this wonderful?" Paul Hayes said, ignoring his squabbling family. With a flourish, he placed a platter of French toast on the table. "Breakfast in the tree room. Served with maple syrup direct from the trees."

"Really?" Alex asked. "Fresh maple syrup? Made today?"

"They make maple syrup in the spring," Isabel explained to him. "When the sap is running, they collect it in buckets under the trees, and then they boil it for hours to make the syrup."

"Spare us the lecture," Eva interrupted.

"Your brain is overoxygenated," Isabel told her.

Abby took a breath. "Could everyone try to be

a little nicer? Hannah's going to be back from the shower any minute."

"Excellent suggestion, Abby," her mother agreed. "Only let's be nice for the sake of being nice. We're on vacation. I'd like everyone to get along and enjoy themselves."

"How can we enjoy anything today?" Isabel said with a shiver. "It's freezing out!! What kind of vacation weather is this, anyway?"

"*Our* vacation weather," Abby said. She wondered if Brianna had blue skies and warm temperatures over her island. It was only a mile or two away, but it probably had a different weather system.

"Can you make that fire hotter, Dad?" Isabel said. "I didn't bring enough warm clothes."

"You can borrow my orange fleece," Eva offered. "It's in my bag."

"I don't want to look like a traffic light!" Isabel said.

"Girls," Olivia Hayes said in a warning voice, "that's enough."

"Good morning!" Hannah said. She was wearing blue jeans, a yellow sweatshirt, and a long red fleece cap over her wet hair.

Last night, Hannah had talked excitedly about the

boat ride for what seemed like hours. Abby had listened in silence. She had gone to sleep wondering if Hannah wished she was with Brianna's family instead of hers. But now, looking at Hannah, with her dripping wet hair, funny-looking fleece cap, and old blue jeans, she felt oddly reassured.

No one who dressed like that would ever be Brianna's best friend. Or even a good friend. No matter how friendly and enthusiastic she was.

"That hat makes you look like Santa Claus," Alex said.

"Ho, ho, ho," Hannah said. "Did you know that showers cost a dollar fifty?"

"We forgot to warn you," Olivia Hayes said. "I hope you had some quarters."

Hannah nodded. "The shower was on a timer. I had just enough time to wash my hair. It was a race between me and the hot water. But I won!"

"Sit down and have some French toast with us, Hannah," Paul Hayes said. "It's nice to see your cheerful face first thing in the morning."

Hannah sat down next to Abby. "What do you want to do today?" she asked.

"It's too cold to go swimming." Abby didn't hide

the relief in her voice. If they weren't at the lake, they wouldn't run into Brianna again.

"Any ideas for how to spend the day?" Olivia Hayes asked.

"There's a historical museum," Isabel began.

"There's a mountain range," Eva said.

"I want to play on my computer," Alex complained.

"This is the great outdoors, Alex," his father said, gesturing toward the trees and the sky and the leaping campfire. "Away from civilization, computers, phones, fax machines, and —"

"Dad, your cell phone's ringing," Isabel said.

"Can I play games on it when you're done talking?" Alex asked.

Paul Hayes grabbed his phone and pushed the TALK button. "Yes?"

"Does anyone want to pick berries?" Olivia Hayes asked. "There's a farm near here where we can get blueberries and raspberries. Then maybe we'll drive into town for lunch. If you're not too full."

Eva and Isabel groaned. "We always spend *hours* picking."

"You love berries," their mother reminded them.

"Me, too," Alex said. "I'm the best picker in the family."

"That's because you don't eat them," Abby said. "You're the only one who doesn't eat more than he picks."

"Hannah?" Olivia asked. "What about you? You get a vote, too."

"Sounds great," Hannah said, as usual.

"We're picking berries, Dad," Isabel said as her father returned to the table.

"Count me out," Paul Hayes said. "I have to run into town and fax something to a client. Can you drop me off?"

His wife frowned. "It's our vacation, Paul!"

"I don't work for a company like you do, Olivia," he said in a tense tone of voice. "No one covers for me."

"You *never* take time off," his wife said, "and here we all are togeth —"

"Who's on dish duty?" Isabel interrupted.

"Me," Hannah said. "I love to wash dishes."

Paul Hayes disappeared into the tent.

His wife pressed her lips together tightly.

A minute ago, everyone had been laughing. Now there was tension in the air.

Abby grabbed a dish towel and began to dry. Why did her parents choose this moment to start an argument? Vacations were supposed to be for relaxing. Sometimes it seemed as if they brought out the worst in people. Or at least the worst in *her* family.

Chapter 8

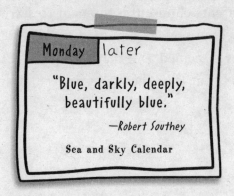

"Blue, darkly, deeply,
beautifully blue."

—*Robert Southey*

Sea and Sky Calendar

And plump, too. A field of fat, ripe purply-blue blueberries, as far as the eye can see. There are billions of them!

"I found a row!" Alex cried. "Over here!"

Abby ignored her younger brother. She had just found a bush laden with blueberries as big as quarters. Next to it was another bush just like it. And another . . .

"Do you think they all taste the same?" Abby asked Hannah. "That's what Eva says."

"No," Hannah said. "Some are sweet, some are tart, some are just —"

"— the essence of blueberry," Abby finished for her. She popped a berry in her mouth and closed her eyes to savor it. "This one is *it*."

"This one is," Hannah contradicted her. "No, this one. *This* one."

"I love this *so* much," Abby said. "Blueberries are *almost* better than pierced ears."

"When we get our ears pierced, we'll have to buy little round blue earrings like blueberries!" Hannah said.

"We'll get matching pairs!" Abby cried. "To remind us of today."

Hannah nodded in agreement.

"How much have you picked?" Isabel demanded from the other side of the bush. She showed them her bucket. "Look at what I've accomplished already."

Abby plunked a few berries into her pail. "I have three berries in my bucket!" she said. "And hundreds in my stomach!"

"Same here," Hannah said. "They're *so* delicious."

Isabel shook her head. "Get serious, you two," she said. "You can't just eat your way through the patch."

"Why not?" Abby asked with a grin. "Sounds like a good idea to me."

She showed Isabel a handful of blueberries. "These are the sweetest berries on earth."

"Put them in your pail," Isabel ordered.

"My mouth," Abby insisted, tipping her head back and spilling the blueberries onto her tongue.

"You'll get a stomachache," Isabel warned. "Don't expect any sympathy from me when you're doubled over in pai —"

"Blueberry paradise!" Abby cried as she tasted the berries. "I've found it!"

"I'm on Blueberry Street," Hannah said.. She waved purple fingertips in the air.

"Mom!" Alex called. "Where are you?"

"Over here!" came a faint cry from several rows over. "I've almost filled a bucket!"

"Mom is faster than anyone," Eva commented. "She and Alex will get most of the berries."

Hannah picked up her pail. "Time to catch up," she announced. "I've eaten plenty, and I'm ready to pick now."

"Abby? Did you hear that?" Isabel demanded.

"Oh, leave her alone," Eva said. "We're going to have too many blueberries, anyway."

Abby glanced at Hannah, who was already filling

her pail. "Oh, all right," she sighed. "I'll stop eating and work, too."

Her sisters were quiet, concentrated on their work.

Abby knelt down to find the plumpest berries at the base of the bush, then went to the next one. After a while, she drifted away from the others.

"It's so chilly!" Isabel complained.

"Did you and Abby swim yesterday?" she asked Hannah.

Hannah nodded. "Not only did we swim, but we went on a boat ride with Brianna."

A few rows away, Abby held her breath and said nothing. She crouched down and picked furiously.

"Brianna?" Eva echoed. "She's here? *Camping?*" Her voice had the same stunned, disbelieving tone that Abby's had the day before.

"She's staying at a summerhouse on an island," Hannah explained.

"Naturally," Isabel said.

"What kind of boat was it?" Eva asked. "A yacht or a cruise ship?"

"It was a motorboat," Hannah said.

"*Only* a motorboat?" Isabel exclaimed. "Was it a new one? The best money can buy?"

"How did you know?" Hannah asked.

Isabel shrugged.

"Brianna always has the best of everything," Eva explained. "It doesn't take a fortune-teller or a genius to predict."

"Hey, I'm both." Isabel playfully punched her twin sister.

"Oh, right," Eva said sarcastically.

Isabel ignored her. She began to tell Hannah about the fortune-telling booth she had manned at the Fall Festival at Lancaster Elementary.

"Hundreds of people came," Isabel said. "And each fortune I told was different. One or two of them even came true."

"*Awesome,*" Hannah said. "Will you tell mine?"

"Woo, woo!" Eva said. "Only the brave ask their fortunes of Madame Is-a-bel!"

"I don't read palms," Isabel said. "And I left my crystal ball at home."

"So?" Hannah said.

"Come on, Isabel!" Eva urged.

"Madame Isabel never disappoints a true seeker." Isabel took Hannah's hand. She traced the lines of her palm. "I see . . . I see . . ."

"I see London, I see France," Eva chanted.

Isabel scowled at her twin. "Shut up, Eva. I see that you are a very friendly person," she said to Hannah. "I see that you will make many friends at Lancaster Elementary. I see that everyone will like you. I see that you will enjoy your new class and neighborhood."

"Thanks!" Hannah said. "That's a great fortune!"

"It will all come true," Isabel predicted.

A few rows away, Abby sighed deeply.

Why hadn't Isabel predicted a new best friend? Why hadn't she predicted one named Abby Hayes?

Chapter 9

Monday evening

"You see things; and you say 'Why?'
But I dream things that never were;
and I say 'Why not?' "
—George Bernard Shaw

Inventors' Daily Planner

<u>My Father's Reaction on Seeing the
Blueberries</u>

(There were six buckets or approximately
twelve gallons.)

"<u>WHY?</u>"

<u>My Mother's Defense of the Blueberries</u>

(She didn't mention they cost more than
sixty dollars.)

"Why <u>not</u>?"

<u>My Mother and Father Discuss the
Blueberries</u>

Paul: What on earth are we going to do with all these berries?

Olivia: Eat them, of course.

Paul: Six buckets' worth? We don't have a refrigerator, a freezer, or a stove. We're at a campsite, not a house.

Olivia: We can cook blueberry pancakes and blueberry French toast and blueberry skillet bread and blueberry kabobs.

Paul: Blueberry <u>kabobs</u>?

Olivia: We'll have to be creative.

Paul: There's enough to feed an army here. How much did you spend on these berries, anyway?

Olivia: The children and I had a <u>very</u> relaxing and pleasant morning at the blueberry farm.

Paul (tensely): I <u>didn't</u> enjoy spending the day in front of a fax machine!

Olivia: Did I say a word?

Paul: I could tell by your tone of voice.

<u>My Mother and Father Don't Discuss the Blueberries; they Argue</u>

71

Never mind what they said.

What happened to the Hayes Peace Proclamation, anyway?

(My parents are worse than my siblings!)

What does Hannah think? She hasn't said a word. I bet Brianna's parents don't fight in front of guests!!!

Isabel and Eva Discuss the Blueberries
Isabel: Good thing we didn't pick rasp-berries, too.

Eva (groans): Don't mention the B word!

Isabel: You ate too many in the car.

Eva: What about you? (Doubles over in sudden pain.) Uh-oh! (Heads toward comfort station at a run.)

Isabel (smugly): That's what she gets for – (Turns pale green, groans, and runs after Eva.)

After Their Return, Eva and Isabel
Discuss the Blueberries Some More

Eva: I'll never eat another of those evil blue things again.

Isabel: Me, neither.

The twins shudder at the sight of thousands of berries on the picnic table.

Eva (suddenly suspicious): Why aren't Abby and Hannah sick? They ate ten times as many as we did!

Isabel (resentful): It's <u>not fair</u>!

Abby: Don't blame us just because we have stomachs made of steel. Right, Hannah?

Hannah: Right!

Eva (irritable): Go ahead and gloat, Abby!

Abby: I am <u>not</u> gloa —

Olivia (stops arguing with husband): It's our vacation, girls. Please don't argue.

Eva: But —

Abby: But —

Olivia: <u>Not another word!</u>

<u>The Family Stands Around the Picnic Table and Gazes at the Blueberries in Despair</u>

Olivia: I hate to think of them going to waste.

Eva: Ugh. Who cares?

Isabel: I wish we had never gone.

Alex: We're drowning in blueberries!

Abby: I wish that we could change them all into pumpkins. Or marshmallows. Or chocolates. Or jelly beans. Or —

Isabel: Will you <u>please</u> stop talking about food?

Paul: This is ridiculous.

Hannah: Why don't we invite lots of people over for a blueberry-eating party?

For a moment, the Hayes family is stunned into silence. Then they all cluster around Hannah to thank her. Isabel and Eva look cheerful for the first time in hours. Alex is jumping up and down. My parents hug each other.

<u>The Family Stands Around the Picnic Table and Gazes at the Blueberries with Renewed Hope</u>

Olivia: We'll have a Celebration of Berries.

Isabel: The celebration comes <u>after</u> they're eaten.

Eva: Whom should we invite?

Hannah (gestures): All the campers.

Abby: Total strangers?

Olivia: Anyone who'll eat these berries is a friend of mine.

Paul: We get rid of the berries and get to know our fellow campers at the same time. The <u>perfect</u> solution.

Hannah: Let's invite Brianna, too.

Olivia: Good idea. It'll be a nice way to thank her family for the boat ride.

Abby (thinking quickly): Brianna doesn't like blueberries.

Olivia: <u>Everyone</u> loves blueberries. Except us right now, of course.

Paul: This will be an interesting evening.

Abby (mutters): Thanks, Dad.

Paul: Don't worry, honey.

Olivia: Where's my cell phone? I'll call

Brianna's family right now. Then Abby and Hannah can invite the neighboring campsites.

Paul: Bring on the blueberry-starved hordes!!

Chapter 10

Thursday morning

"When life hands you lemons, make lemonade."

Illustrated Citrus Almanac

When life hands you blueberries, make friends.

    Blueberries left: 0
    Friends made: 27
    Fun had: Quite a bit
    Instruments brought to party: 3 (a fiddle, a guitar, and an accordion)
    Songs played: A lot
    Laughter heard: Continuous
    Unwanted guests (you know who): 0

* * *

Those zeros should be smiling faces!! <u>Hooray!!</u> I'm glad that Brianna never showed up. And that we have no more blueberries to fight over.

Will give Hannah a page in <u>Hayes Book of World Records</u> for Superb Stomach-Saving Suggestion.

She also gets a special mention as Hayes Family Holiday Hero. Why do I worry about my family fighting in front of Hannah? They stop fighting when she's around. Everyone loves her.

But does she love us? Or <u>me</u>?

"Ready, everyone?" Paul Hayes said.

Abby swung her backpack onto her back. Inside, she had packed a fleece jacket, a hat, a compass, a Swiss army knife, a raincoat in its own pouch, a flashlight, her journal and purple pen, and a few sandwiches for when they reached the top of the mountain.

"It's a day hike, Abby, not a weeklong expedition," Isabel said.

"So?" Abby said.

"You'll have to carry that pack all day long," Eva pointed out.

"My school backpack weighs at least fifty pounds more," Abby retorted.

"That's true," her mother agreed.

"I brought my lunch," Hannah said, "the most important thing of all. And suntan lotion. And a bandanna."

"You won't get burned in the forest," Isabel said. "Or anywhere else today."

The weather had been cold and rainy yesterday. And cold and cloudy the day before that. And cold and windy the day before.

Hannah didn't complain much, but everyone else did.

"It's warmer than yesterday," Abby said to her sister. "Look on the bright side."

"Bright? It's been cloudy, cloudy, and cloudy," Eva grumbled. "I'm glad that we're spending the day in town."

"I'm glad that we're *not* spending the day in town," Paul Hayes said. "It's a perfect day for mountain climbing. Right, Alex?"

"Right, Dad!" Alex said. He was wearing jeans, a T-shirt, and sneakers. His baseball cap was perched at an odd angle on his head.

"You're sure you don't want to come with us?" Paul Hayes asked his wife and the twins.

All three shook their heads.

"The twins and I have a full day planned that includes shopping and eating out," Olivia said. "Enjoy yourselves on the mountain. We'll see you at five o'clock."

"Bear Mountain is my favorite place to hike," Paul Hayes told Alex, Abby, and Hannah as they stepped onto the trail. "I've been coming here since I was a teenager."

Abby tried to imagine her father as a teenager and failed. "Were you like Eva or Isabel?" she asked.

"I was a teenage boy, not a teenage girl," Paul pointed out.

Abby rolled her eyes. "I *know* that, Dad!"

"Did you like sports, like Eva?" Alex asked. "Or school, like Isabel?"

"I liked hiking in the woods," Paul Hayes said. "And playing clarinet. I was much quieter than the two of them. Maybe I was more like Abby."

"Me?" Abby said in surprise. Her father often seemed to understand her when no one else did. Maybe that was why.

"You kind of look alike," Hannah said.

"Except Dad doesn't have wild, curly red hair," Abby pointed out.

"What about you, Hannah?" Paul asked. "Who are you like? Your mom or your dad?"

"I'm tall, like my dad," Hannah said, "and I like to swim, like my mom. I'm curious, like my dad, and friendly, like my mom. I guess I'm like both of them."

"What's your favorite subject?" Alex asked. "Or sport or color?"

"Everything," Hannah said, with a smile. "I like the rainbow, all sports, and all subjects."

"Phew," Alex said. "That's a *lot*!"

"We know what Abby likes," her father teased.

"Writing, Ms. Bunder, purple, Rollerblading, soccer, my journal, and my room," Abby recited.

She wondered if her father and Alex noticed that Jessica's name was no longer on the list.

"Awesome," Hannah said.

Abby glanced quickly at her. Did she really mean that?

"Tell me about Ms. Bunder," Hannah said.

"She's the *best*." Abby began to describe Ms. Bunder's creative writing class.

"She'd make up an assignment from this hike!" Abby concluded. "Ms. Bunder turns everything into cool writing assignments."

"Wow," Hannah said. "That's incredible."

"*She* is," Abby said.

Paul Hayes was in his own world. With a faraway look in his eyes, he gazed at a stand of birch trees. "I used to pick up pieces of birch bark from the ground and write messages on them with sticks."

"We could write poems," Abby said to Hannah.

"Or messages for other campers," Hannah added.

"So long as you don't strip the bark from the trees," Abby's father cautioned. "That hurts them."

"We'll pick up bark from the ground," Abby promised. "If we can find any."

Paul pointed toward a rocky cliff just above them. "Do you know that there are caves in those rocks? Bears live there."

"Bears?" Hannah repeated. "Here? In the woods? Will we see them?"

"Probably not," Paul said. "They appear mostly at

dawn and twilight. We'll be back at the campsite long before dusk."

"Good," Hannah said.

"Once a bear appeared at the campsite where Abby's mom and I were camping," Paul said. "I banged pots and pans together to let it know that we were there. It was looking for food. We had to hang our food from the trees every night."

"How come we don't see any bears at our camp-site?" Abby asked.

"Too many people," her father said.

"*Good*," Hannah said again.

Paul picked up a long, stout stick. "The perfect walking stick," he said with satisfaction. "Now I can hike with confidence."

Alex picked up another stick. "Me, too."

Hannah and Abby began to laugh. "That stick is bigger than you, Alex!"

"*So?*" Alex said. He hurried after his father.

"Your little brother is cute," Hannah said.

"So is your little sister," Abby answered. She scrambled up a short incline.

Ahead of them, Paul Hayes stopped and waited for everyone to catch up. "There's a hidden path nearby. Follow me!"

They plunged into the forest.

The new path was narrower and harder to see. The forest was deeper and more dense. They walked in silence, accompanied by the sound of the wind in the leaves.

"I think we turn here," Paul Hayes said after a while. "Or is it here?"

"Dad! Don't get us lost!" Abby cautioned.

"Have I ever gotten anyone lost?" her father said. "I forget reservations, but I *never* get lost." He turned to the right. "Besides, I've been up this mountain hundreds of times."

A few moments later he added, "It's been a few years."

"If we stay on the trail, we'll be okay," Abby pointed out. "We're bound to end up *somewhere*."

"You're right, Abby. Spoken like a true woodswoman." Paul Hayes nodded approvingly at her. "The trouble is, I haven't seen a trail marker in a while."

Hannah looked at Abby in alarm.

"I'm sure we've strayed only a few feet from our path," Paul said reassuringly. "Let's stay together and search for a marker. Everything will be all right."

Chapter 11

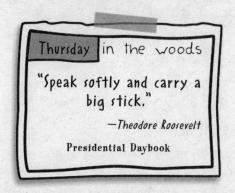

Thursday in the woods

"Speak softly and carry a big stick."

—Theodore Roosevelt

Presidential Daybook

Dad is doing both.

He is speaking very carefully, very slowly, and very gently.

So he won't alarm anyone? So Alex won't start crying? So Hannah and I won't get scared?

Dad is also carrying a big walking stick and using it to lead the way. Sometimes he uses it to get past brambles and thorns.

We are lost. Really lost. We've been searching for more than an hour and haven't found a trail marker. Or any sign of a trail. We have no idea where we are or what to do.

Our cell phone can't pick up a signal here, so we can't call for help.

Dad is pretending that everything is okay. But I know it isn't.

"Time for a break," Paul Hayes said. He pulled a bandanna out of his backpack and wiped the sweat from his face.

He turned to Abby, Alex, and Hannah and tried to smile. "We're having an adventure, aren't we?" he said.

Alex and Hannah didn't say anything. Hannah had taken off her sneakers and was rubbing her feet. Alex curled up around his backpack and closed his eyes.

"Sure, Dad," Abby said wearily.

She wanted to ask how lost they were and what would happen if they couldn't find their way out of the woods.

But she didn't say anything. Her father looked too worried.

"How long have we been out here?" Hannah asked.

No one answered.

Alex sat up. "I'm hungry," he said. He opened his backpack and took out a sandwich.

"I want to be back at the campsite," Hannah said.

"Dad will get us home," Abby said. She spoke softly, like her father had done.

A blue jay flew through the trees and landed on a branch above their heads.

Alex put down his uneaten sandwich. "Why don't we start a fire so someone can find us?"

Paul Hayes sighed. "We'd have to be *very* careful. Maybe later. Besides, did anyone bring matches?"

"I have an electronic game," Alex said. "And a package of gum and three rocks."

His father sat down on a rock and unzipped his backpack. "I have a map. If we could just figure out where we are."

"I have a compass," Abby said. "Will that help?"

Paul Hayes sprang to his feet. "Abby!" He snatched the compass, then hugged and kissed his daughter. "You're a genius!"

Abby glanced over at Hannah to see if she had heard.

"Does this mean we'll find the trail?" Hannah asked.

"Now we have a much better chance," Paul said, settling down to study the map again.

He checked the position of the sun. He looked at the compass and stared at the map.

"We need to go that way," he said, finally, pointing to a densely wooded area.

Holding the compass in his right hand, Paul Hayes led the way through overgrown brush, thorny bushes, and deep forest.

It was dark in the forest, almost like twilight.

"When will we be out of here?" Hannah whispered to Abby.

Abby stepped over a rotting log. "Soon," she said. "In a little while."

She hoped it was true.

"Are there bears in the woods?" Hannah asked.

"Oh, *yeah*," Alex said.

Hannah turned pale.

"It's okay," Abby reassured her. "I'm sure we won't see any. Bears are very shy creatures."

"If they come close, don't scream or make high-pitched noises," Paul Hayes said. "Talk normally and wave your arms."

"The bear will eat me first," Alex said cheerfully.

"Oh!" Hannah cried.

Abby gave her brother a not-so-gentle push. "Shut *up*, Alex!" She turned to Hannah. "Dad knows what to do. He'll protect us."

"Thanks for the vote of confidence," Paul said. He stopped and consulted the compass.

"This way!" he said, pointing to a sloping ravine. "Straight down!"

"Straight down?" Hannah repeated. Her voice trembled a little.

"Nothing to it. Watch me." Paul attached his walking stick to his backpack. Then, sliding sideways and using trees like poles to balance himself, he descended rapidly to the base of the ravine.

"Come on!" he called. "It's not hard!"

Alex sat down and scooted like a crab to the bottom.

Hannah took a few wobbly steps forward, then flung her arms around a young sapling.

"Walk sideways," Abby coached her. "Try to get to the next tree."

Hannah put one foot forward and began to slide. She clung to a tree, slid again, clung, and stumbled.

Paul Hayes caught her as she tumbled down. "Are you all right?" he asked.

"You did it!" Abby cried.

Hannah tried to smile.

"I ripped my pants," Alex announced. He turned to show off a large, jagged hole in the seat of his jeans.

"*Dinosaur* underwear?" Abby said.

"Alex's pants are ventilated," Paul Hayes joked.

"They're air-conditioned pants," Abby said. "Maybe you should patent them, Alex."

"If we ever get out of here!" Alex groaned.

The wind suddenly picked up. Treetops swayed and branches creaked. The sky turned darker.

"Let's get going," Paul said, his expression suddenly serious. "To the right."

Rain began to fall from the sky.

"At least it's dry under the trees," Abby said. "We have a canopy of leaves to protect us."

"A tree umbrella," Alex began.

"That doesn't weigh an ounce," Abby finished, "because the trees are holding it up for us."

"Ouch!" Alex stumbled over a tree root and fell down. He got back up and pointed to his pant knee. "Ripped again," he said sadly.

"Just don't break any bones," his father said. "I can't carry you out of here."

"Let's guess how many times Alex will rip his pants today," Abby suggested.

No one laughed at her joke. Just then, Hannah slipped on a patch of wet leaves and lost her balance. She flung her arms out and crashed into Abby.

The two of them swayed, bumped into each other again, and toppled over.

"Okay, Hannah?" Paul Hayes asked, with a worried look. "Abby?"

"Yes," Hannah said in a small voice, getting to her feet.

"Alive," Abby said, brushing off her clothes. "Nothing torn or broken."

"Five-minute rest stop," Paul announced. "Let's all take a breath. We're tired, and that's when accidents happen."

"Where *are* we?" Alex asked. "This looks like the place we left an hour ago."

"We're following the compass," Paul Hayes said, "and the direction of the sun."

"The sun has disappeared," Abby said, gazing at the dark, ominous sky.

"We have to keep going," Paul insisted. "Otherwise — "

Thunder rumbled in the sky. There was a flash of lightning, and it began to pour.

Chapter 12

Thursday (again), raining (more)

"There is really no such thing as bad weather, only different kinds of good weather."
—*John Ruskin*
Hurricane, Monsoon, and Typhoon Calendar

Oh, <u>yeah</u>? Did he ever get lost in the woods in a thunderstorm? Did he have to march over slippery leaves and rocks with the rain pouring into his face and not knowing where he was going? Did he ever wonder if he was hopelessly lost and would have to spend the night in the woods with bears and other wild animals lurking nearby, in soaking wet clothes, without a fire? Did he realize that his friend would probably never speak to him again in her life, if they ever got out of there? Did he have to watch her crying and stumbling over rocks and roots?

<u>Did he???</u>

If John Ruskin had been on our family vacation, he would have written: "There is really no such thing as good weather, only different kinds of bad weather."

We now pause to calm down for a minute.

It was raining so hard that I almost forgot that I had brought a raincoat. I pulled it out of my backpack and gave it to Hannah. She was quietly crying. She had been crying for a while. She was continuing to cry. She might never stop crying. Nothing I said or did was of any help at all.

Before Camping Trip
Hannah smiled nonstop.

After Camping Trip

Hannah cried nonstop.

<u>What have we done to Hannah?</u> She
<u>used to be the world's most cheerful and</u>
<u>happy person!!!!</u>

Dad spotted a sheltered area under a
rocky overhang. We stopped to get out of
the rain for a short while.

Under the Dry Rock

1. Dad: consulting soggy
map
2. Alex: unwrapping
soggy bubble gum
3. Hannah: rubbing
soggy eyes
4. Abby: writing in
soggy journal

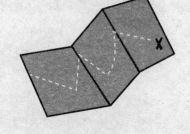

It's six P.M. Mom, Eva, and Isabel must
be wondering where we are. Maybe they've
called the park police or the forest rangers.
Is someone going to rescue us?

Or do they think we've stopped for dinner? Will they wait until dark before they call for help? Or until tomorrow morning?

Dad just left to scout the area. We are calling back and forth so he won't get lost.
This is what we are yelling:
"Hey!"
"Hey!"
"Ho!"
"Hey!"
"Hooooo!" (Alex, trying to imitate an owl.)
"Hey!"
"Hey!"
"Dad?"
"Dad!!!"
"DAD!"

"Boo," Dad said, appearing suddenly. He was dripping wet and smiling.
"That's not funny," Alex protested.
Dad was in a good mood. "I found a stream!" he announced.
No one was impressed.

"More water," I said. "Great."

"A stream is like a road," Dad explained. "We can follow it."

"To where?" Hannah asked.

"I don't know," Dad admitted, "but we won't be going in circles. If I'm right, it'll lead us straight out of here."

We are going to follow the stream.

Is following a stream like following your heart? My heart knows where I want to go but not how to get there. The stream is going someplace, but I don't know where.

Dad has already gotten us lost several times today. Maybe this time he'll get us found?

Chapter 13

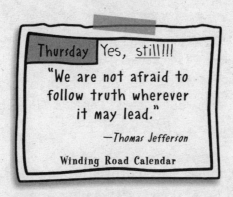

Thursday Yes, still!!!

"We are not afraid to
follow truth wherever
it may lead."

—Thomas Jefferson

Winding Road Calendar

We are not afraid to follow Dad wherever he may lead.

(Actually, we have no choice.)

Dad is leading us out of the woods.
Dad is leading us to a road.
Dad is leading us to a house.

Our feet are sore, our legs are tired, our
arms are scratched. We're wet and cold,
but we're back in civilization.

In a little while we'll be wearing dry
clothes and eating hot food.

Our tent will seem like a palace. We'll have flush toilets and showers nearby. Mom will build a fire. Our neighbors will be humans.

Three cheers for Dad!!! Hooray! Hooray! Hooray!

The forest ranger's Jeep drove through the state park and pulled up at the Hayes family campsite.

"Thank you again," Paul said to the forest ranger.

"I'm glad you didn't have to spend the night outdoors in this rain," she replied.

It was dark out. The campsite looked deserted. The rain was falling hard on the tents, the van, and the picnic table.

"Where is everyone?" Alex asked.

Dad shook his head. "I don't know." He opened the door of the Jeep and stepped out into the rain. "Maybe they're at the office, waiting for news."

The Jeep drove away.

For a moment, they all stood in the rain.

Then Paul Hayes sprang into action. He opened the door of the van and found umbrellas and plastic bags.

He gave the girls a handful of quarters. "Abby and Hannah, take long, hot showers, and change into dry clothes. Put your wet, dirty clothes in these bags. Alex and I will do the same. After we're warm and dry, we'll find your mother and sisters."

The girls trudged back to the campsite in silence.

Already their feet were wet and cold again, squishing through the soaked grass.

As they approached the campsite, Abby's mother ran out to greet them.

"You're back! You're safe! You're alive!" Olivia hugged Abby first and then Hannah over and over.

"The twins and I went to the park office," she explained. "We were trying to find out what happened to you."

"Dad led us out of the wilderness," Abby said. "If he hadn't, we would have spent the night in the pouring rain."

Hannah shuddered.

"Are you okay, Hannah?" Olivia asked. "It must have been really tough on you. Your first time, too! Hikes aren't usually like this."

Abby glanced gratefully at her mother.

"I'm okay." Hannah drew a long, shaky breath. "Just sore and tired."

Olivia put her arms around both girls. "I am *so* proud of both of you. What a day! What an adventure! We were so worried when you didn't show up at five o'clock. Thank goodness you're all right."

They arrived at the campsite. No one was in sight.

"Where are they *now*?" Olivia asked anxiously. "I wish your father wouldn't keep disappearing."

The window of the van opened. Paul was sitting in the front seat. Alex, Isabel, and Eva were behind him.

Abby and Hannah began to laugh.

"They didn't go far, Mom," Abby said.

"Get in the car," Paul said, smiling.

"Why? Where? Haven't we had enough adventure?" Olivia protested.

"We're taking a vacation from our vacation," Paul announced. "I've reserved some rooms in a nearby lodge."

"*Two* hot showers in one night?" Alex said.

"Maybe I'll take three," Abby said as she stepped out of the bathroom in her mother's bathrobe and a thick towel wrapped around her head.

"Me, too," Hannah chimed in. "I'm taking another shower before bed."

"One is enough for me!" Alex declared.

"Take as many hot showers as you want," Olivia said. "And make sure you drink plenty of hot chocolate, too," she added. "We want you warm and toasty, inside and out."

"Okay," Abby agreed. She sat down on the couch next to her brother.

The rooms in the lodge were equipped with microwaves, hot plates, refrigerators, and television sets. The family had gathered in the girls' room to watch TV and eat popcorn, while Paul went out to pick up Chinese food.

"The luxuries of civilization!" Isabel proclaimed, taking a handful of popcorn.

"After we eat, I'm going to lie in bed, listen to the rain, and read a novel," Olivia announced.

"Television!" Alex cried.

"This is my kind of camping," Eva said, stretching out on the floor.

"I can't believe you said that," Isabel said. "You're usually tougher than the rest of the world!"

Eva shrugged. "This is for Abby and Hannah and Alex. They've been through so much today."

"Dad said they were brave," Isabel added.

"He did?" Abby couldn't believe her ears.

"Especially when lightning struck, trees crashed to the ground next to us, and then bears attacked," Alex began.

"Pass the popcorn and don't exaggerate," Isabel said.

Hannah shuddered. "Bears!"

"I saw a bear up close once," Olivia said. "I was so scared I couldn't move."

"What did you do?" Alex asked.

"Nothing. The bear went away. Your father wasn't frightened at all."

"Is camping always like this?" Hannah asked in a small voice.

"This is the deluxe trip," Eva joked. "You should see what happens when we rough it."

"Have *you* ever gotten lost, Eva?" Isabel demanded.

"At least I'm not permanently lost, like you," Eva retorted.

"Girls," Olivia sighed.

The door opened. Paul Hayes entered, carrying bags of food.

"Dinner is served," he announced, taking fragrant,

steaming containers from their bags and placing them on the table. "Help yourself, because I'm too tired to help you."

He sank down in a chair and yanked his baseball cap over his face.

"Dad!" Abby said in embarrassment.

"We hiked eighteen miles today," Paul mumbled from underneath the cap. "We went around the mountain instead of up it."

"Eighteen miles," Hannah repeated in wonder. "I've never walked more than three miles in my life."

"Me, neither," Abby said.

Paul sat up. "You kids were the greatest," he said. "You hardly even complained."

"We were? We didn't?" Abby and Hannah glanced at each other.

"I couldn't have gotten us out without your help," Paul said. He leaned back in the chair and closed his eyes again. "Or without the compass," he added.

"I ripped my jeans in two places," Alex bragged. "I'm going to wear them on the first day of school."

"You better wear a second pair of jeans underneath," Abby warned him.

"Let's eat now," Eva said impatiently. "We can talk later. That food smells good!"

"Abby, Alex, and Hannah, go first," Olivia said.

Abby stood up. "Are you hungry?" she asked Hannah.

"I'm *starved*! I could eat a horse!"

"You'll have to make do with chicken, shrimp, and tofu," Paul said sleepily.

Chapter 14

Thursday ~~Not anymore!~~

"Home again, home again,
jiggety jog."

Little Piggies Calendar

We're back!!

Before heading home, we dropped Hannah off. Her whole family came out to greet her.

Her little sister, Elena, is so cute!!

Elena hugged Hannah and said, "Mommy, Mommy." That means "pick me up."

She gave Hannah a pair of sunglasses shaped like daisies and made Hannah put them on. Hannah looked funny!

❀   ❀   ❀

Her parents haven't found a place to live yet.

"The pressure is on," Hannah's dad said.

Hannah groaned. "More boxes to pack?"

"Lots more," her mother said. "<u>And</u> we have five appointments tomorrow to look at houses."

"Ugh," Hannah said. "I wish I were back on Bear Mountain."

"You <u>do</u>?" I said in amazement.

"Well, actually, no," Hannah said.

"You climbed Bear Mountain?" her father asked. "I'm impressed."

"Sort of," Hannah mumbled.

My father spoke up. "I got everyone lost," he admitted. "We wandered around the woods for a while—"

"—and then we took a vacation from the vacation," Hannah cried. "It was so much fun! And we swam, went on a motorboat ride, picked gallons of berries, threw a blueberry eating party, and—"

"It sounds like a dozen vacations in one," her mother commented.

"It was <u>great</u>!" Hannah said.

* * *

Hannah's smile is back! Hooray!!! I'm glad she's not angry or upset about Bear Mountain. I'm glad she liked camping. I'm glad she and I are still friends. I'm <u>almost</u> sorry that the trip is over.

Monday two weeks later

"Never laugh at live dragons."

—J. R. R. Tolkien

Great Big Calendar of
Little Tiny Things

Okay, I won't.

There is nothing else to say about this quote. And I know it doesn't make any sense! Does it <u>have</u> to?

Guess what? I went to sleep-away camp for two weeks! We slept on beds in cabins. The weather was hot and sunny. We swam every day and canoed, kayaked, and sailed. We never got lost in the mountains. I didn't worry about anything.

Things I DIDN'T Worry About

1. If my friends were having a good time or not.
2. Will I ever find another best friend?
3. Does Friend A like Friend B better than me?

Hooray! Hooray! Hooray!

The only bad thing that happened was: I FORGOT TO BRING MY JOURNAL!!!
Boo-hoo. Boo-hoo. Boo-hoo!
Sorry, Journal. I really missed you. And I'm so glad to see you again.

Hannah didn't call while I was gone. I wonder if they've found a house yet.

"I have to buy colored folders, an eraser, glue, scissors, wide-ruled paper, crayons, colored pencils, and a box of tissues," Abby recited.

Yesterday she had received a list of school supplies in the mail. Now she and her father were at OfficeParadise.

"I'll pick up the tissues," her father said. "You get everything else. I'll meet you in the computer aisle."

"Okay, Dad," Abby said.

Paul Hayes hurried away. Abby selected two purple pens for writing in her journal and a package of six black pens for schoolwork.

"These glitter gel pens are the coolest," said a familiar voice.

"I bought, like, six in every color," said another familiar voice. "So I could have like, you know, matching school supplies."

"Even the tissues?" Abby asked.

Brianna and Victoria stood behind her. They were dressed in shimmery shirts and tiny skirts. Brianna wore colored lip gloss. Victoria's eyelids were pale green.

"Like, everything's coordinated," Victoria continued, ignoring Abby's comment. "My lipstick, my shoes, and my glitter pens."

Brianna frowned. "Mine, too!" She pointed to her ears. "I've coordinated my earrings with my binder and erasers."

"Like, who ever heard of matched earrings and *erasers*?" Victoria asked scornfully.

"My cousins on the island match *everything*," Brianna retorted. "You know, we spent practically the entire summer on the island."

She turned to Abby. "Remember our private island?"

Now it was Victoria's turn to frown. "*My* family traveled to Los Angeles. We, like — "

"We cruised the lake on our motorboat," Brianna interrupted. "Abby and Hannah took a ride with us. It was the coolest."

"There was a very cool breeze," Abby agreed.

"Hannah?" Victoria asked, suddenly jealous. "Like, who is *she*?"

"She's the best" — Brianna began, then stopped — "Look! There she is! Hannah!" she called. "Over here!"

Hannah hurried toward them. Her eyes were sparkling. She was smiling at all three girls.

Abby had forgotten how cheerful Hannah was. It made her feel cheerful, too, just to see her.

Brianna introduced her. "Hannah, Victoria. Victoria, Hannah. Now you've met. Two of the coolest girls in fifth grade."

"Hi!" Hannah said.

Victoria stared at Hannah. "She's cool?" she said to Brianna. "Like, *why*?"

Brianna ignored Victoria. "I can't wait until you're in our class," she said to Hannah.

"Me, neither!" Hannah said.

"You'll get to see me perform in the holiday play," Brianna said. "I'm a professional, you know. I've been on TV."

"Awesome," Hannah said.

"Well, it's been, like, *nice* to meet you, Hannah," Victoria said sarcastically. "But we have to, like, shop, you know."

"I have my own credit card," Brianna bragged.

"Wow," Hannah said.

Abby frowned. Was Hannah going to say "Yay, Brianna!" next?

"Come *on*!" Victoria tugged Brianna's arm. "There are, like, twelve sales today."

Brianna waved airily at Abby and Hannah. "Au revoir!"

"Orey — where?" Hannah said.

"It means good-bye in French," Abby explained. Everyone learned French when Brianna was around.

The two girls were silent for a moment.

"Is Victoria always like — ?"

"You mean, like, always like, you know, like . . ."

Hannah nodded.

"Victoria's like that."

"Brianna?" Hannah asked. "Does she *always* — "

"I thought you liked her," Abby said in surprise.

"I like *everyone*," Hannah said. "But — "

"But?"

"*But,*" Hannah said again. It seemed to be the final word on Brianna.

She took a breath. "Guess what? We found a house."

"You did!" Abby cried.

"If Ms. Kantor asks what we did on our summer vacation, I'm going to say packing and unpacking." Hannah groaned. "I never want to see another cardboard box in my life!"

"It sounds awful," Abby said in sympathy.

"If it wasn't for camping with your family, my whole summer would have been a waste!"

"For real?" Abby said.

"I *loved* the vacation vacation," Hannah said. "Eating Chinese food and watching movies."

"We both fell asleep in the middle of the movie," Abby reminded her.

"It was still fun," Hannah said.

"But what about Bear Mountain?" Abby asked. "That was a disaster!"

Hannah thought for a moment. "You helped me when I was scared."

"It was nothing."

"You were always watching out for me," Hannah continued. "And *you* weren't scared at all."

Abby didn't know what to say. She grabbed a pair of scissors from the display and put them in her basket.

Hannah seemed embarrassed, too. "I have to get school supplies," she said, pulling a crumpled list from her pocket.

"Matching gel pens and erasers?" Abby said.

"Huh?"

"Brianna and Victoria are coordinating all their school supplies," Abby explained.

The two girls began to laugh.

"Oh, hi, Hannah!" Paul Hayes said, walking quickly toward the girls. His basket held computer paper, cables, and blank CDs.

"Hi!" Hannah greeted him. "Guess what? We found a house. It's at the corner of Maple and Yates."

"That's near us!" Abby cried.

Hannah nodded. "We wanted to stop by and say hello," she said, "but with preparing for the new school year, *and* moving, *and* shopping — "

"It sounds *very* hectic," Paul commented. "Do you want to have dinner with us tonight?"

"*Yes!*" Hannah cried, glancing at Abby. "All I've eaten for a week is grilled cheese sandwiches and tacos," she added.

"Just what we're planning for this evening," Paul joked. "I'm kidding, Hannah! Don't look so alarmed. It'll be a five-course dinner, with no blueberries."

"Raspberries?" Hannah said. "Blackberries? Strawberries?"

"Neapolitan ice cream," Paul said. "With chocolate sauce."

"Yum," Hannah said.

Abby took a breath. "Can Hannah stay overnight, too?" she asked. "For a sleepover?"

"If it's okay with her parents."

Hannah's face lit up. "I'd love to! My mom will say yes. She *better*."

Abby sighed with happiness.

It was going to be the best school year yet, she thought.

FROM

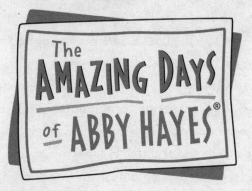

The
AMAZING DAYS
of **ABBY HAYES**®

12: Good Things Come in Small Packages

COMING SOON

That's what Ms. Kantor told us yester-day. As a special project for the holidays, our class will make small packages of good things. We will send them to kids whose families can't afford presents. Ms. Kantor suggested that each of us fill a shoe box with toys, games, puzzles, or clothing items like socks or mittens.

Next week, we'll each bring a shoe box to school and decorate it with colored paper. Then we'll fill the boxes with good things, and Ms. Kantor will deliver them.

Hooray! Lots of kids will have happier holidays because of our small packages. And our holidays will be happier, too.

A double hooray!!! Because today is Thursday. It is finally time for creative writing again. I can't wait to see Ms. Bunder! What will she assign us today?

"We're going to try something different," Ms. Bunder announced. The creative-writing teacher was wearing an orange sweater with a beaded flower design and white pants.

"She looks like an ice-cream cone," Hannah whispered to Abby. "Orange sherbet and vanilla ice cream."

"With sprinkles," Natalie added, pointing to the beaded flowers.

Natalie's short dark hair was messy, as if she had just run her hands through it. She wore one turquoise sock and one pink sock. Her fingers had smears of paint and ink on them. Once she had been one of

Abby's best friends. They were still good friends, but Natalie now spent a lot of time with Bethany.

"I love sprinkles!" Hannah exclaimed.

"Me, too—" Natalie began.

"Ssshh," Abby interrupted. "I want to hear Ms. Bunder — "

". . . divide into groups," Ms. Bunder was saying, "and listen to one another read."

"Read what?" Abby looked over at Mason. "Did you hear what she said?"

Mason didn't answer. He pretended to pick his nose.

"Thanks a lot," Abby said. She raised her hand. "Ms. Bunder? Could you repeat that?"

"We're going to read our writing assignments to one another in small groups," Ms. Bunder said. She added, "And then we're going to give feedback."

The fifth-graders looked at one another in alarm.

"Feedback?" Tyler said. "Isn't that something that happens with loudspeakers?"

"It's constructive criticism," Ms. Bunder explained. "Building up, not tearing down. We're going to help one another become better writers."

"What if someone's piece stinks?" Mason asked.

"Mine won't," Brianna announced. "Everyone

will think mine is the best. *Oui, oui*?" she added in French.

"'Weee, weee,' said the Three Little Pigs," Natalie muttered.

"First of all, find something good to say about each person's writing," Ms. Bunder said. "If there's something you don't like, try to explain in a helpful way."

"Instead of 'That's terrible,' say, 'That's terrible because it's boring'?" Zach suggested.

Ms. Bunder smiled. "How would you feel if I said that to you, Zach?"

"Oh, fine," Zach said.

Brianna's hand shot into the air. "You should say, 'Put more excitement and action into your piece. . . .'"

"Yes!" Ms. Bunder agreed.

"The way I do," Brianna concluded triumphantly.

"What about, 'I like the way you describe people, but you should have something happen in your story'?" Abby said.

"Perfect!" Ms. Bunder said.

"Great," Hannah whispered.

Abby blushed. Mason stuck out his tongue at her.

Brianna tossed her hair over her shoulder and sighed dramatically. "My explanation was more perfect."

The creative-writing teacher picked up a stack of

papers and began to pass them out. "I think you all understand what's expected. You're ready to be part of a real writer's group."

"And so ends the marvelous and wonderful story of me," Brianna concluded with a flourish. She put down her paper and looked around the group expectantly.

"Um . . ." Abby began, then fell silent.

Natalie stared at the floor.

Bethany swung her foot back and forth.

Mason burped.

"Well?" Brianna demanded.

There was an uncomfortable silence.

"You have dramatic flair," Hannah said suddenly. "Your story has lots of drama in it."

Everyone in the group breathed a sigh of relief.

Brianna looked pleased. "My life is drama. I play the lead in every play."

"Really?" Hannah said.

"Except when I do," Natalie corrected. She had competed against Brianna and won the lead role in the school play.

Brianna frowned at Natalie. "That was a mis —" she began.

"Are there any other characters in your story?" Abby interrupted. "It's all about you."

"Of course it is," Brianna said.

"You ought to write about animals," Bethany said. "Like hamsters."

"I know that's what you wrote about," Brianna said scornfully.

"Hamsters are lovable and intelligent, especially Blondie —" Bethany began to defend her beloved pet.

"Oh, really?" Brianna said. "You believe that?"

Bethany's eyes narrowed. Her face turned red. "I—"

"Did you write about your hamster, Bethany?" Hannah interrupted. "I love hamsters! Will you read next?"

Bethany looked pleased. "Some people appreciate the animal kingdom," she said to no one in particular.

"I love hamsters, too," Natalie said. "Remember?"

"Hamsters!" Brianna said in exasperation. Scowling, she took a mirror from her purse and applied colored gloss to her lips.

"Show-off!" Bethany mumbled.

"Read your story," Hannah urged her again.

Bethany picked up her paper and began to read. " 'Blondie: Life of a Hamster . . .'"

"Hannah saves the day," Natalie whispered to Abby.

Abby nodded proudly.

Everyone liked Hannah — even Brianna. Hannah never made enemies — only more and more friends. And Abby was her first friend.

MORE SERIES YOU'LL FALL IN LOVE WITH

GET READY FOR GABi!

Gabi is a lucky girl. She can speak English *and* Spanish. But some days, when things get crazy, Gabi's words get all mixed-up!

Jody is about to begin a dream vacation on the wide-open sea, traveling to new places and helping her parents with their dolphin research. You can tag along with

Dolphin Diaries

Heartland™

Nestled in the foothills of Virginia, there's a place where horses come when they are hurt. Amy, Ty, and everyone at Heartland work together to heal the horses—and form lasting bonds that will touch your heart.

Learn more at
www.scholastic.com/books

Available Wherever Books Are Sold.

GIRL